A Note to Parents

Eyewitness Readers is a compelling new program for beginning readers, designed in conjunction with leading literacy experts, including Dr. Linda Gambrell, President of the National Reading Conference and past board member of the International Reading Association.

Eyewitness has become the most trusted name in illustrated books, and this new series combines the highly visual *Eyewitness* approach with engaging, easy-to-read stories. Each *Eyewitness Reader* is guaranteed to capture a child's interest while developing his or her reading skills, general knowledge, and love of reading.

The four levels of *Eyewitness Readers* are aimed at different reading abilities, enabling you to choose the books that are exactly right for your children:

Level 1, for **Preschool to Grade 1**
Level 2, for **Grades 1 to 3**
Level 3, for **Grades 2 and 3**
Level 4, for **Grades 2 to 4**

The "normal" age at which a child begins to read can be anywhere from three to eight years old, so these levels are intended only as a general guideline.

No matter which level you select, you can be sure that you are helping your child learn to read, then read to learn!

A DK PUBLISHING BOOK
www.dk.com

Project Editor Penny Smith
Art Editor Susan Calver
Senior Editor Linda Esposito
Senior Art Editor Diane Thistlethwaite
US Editor Regina Kahney
Production Melanie Dowland
Picture Researcher Andrea Sadler
Jacket Designer Margherita Gianni
Illustrator Chris Forsey
Index Lynn Bresler

Reading Consultant
Linda B. Gambrell, Ph.D.

First American Edition, 2000
2 4 6 8 10 9 7 5 3 1
Published in the United States by DK Publishing, Inc.
95 Madison Avenue, New York, New York 10016

Published in Great Britain by Dorling Kindersley Limited.

Eyewitness Readers™ is a trademark of
Dorling Kindersley Limited, London.

Library of Congress Cataloging-in-Publication Data

Bull, Angela, 1936-
 Flying ace : the story of Amelia Earhart / by Angela Bull. -- 1st American ed.
  p. cm. -- (Dorling Kindersley readers)
 Summary: Examines the life and disappearance of the pilot who was the first woman to
cross the Atlantic in a plane by herself.
 ISBN 0-7894-5436-X (hc.) -- ISBN 0-7894-5435-1 (pb.)
 1. Earhart, Amelia, 1897-1937--Juvenile literature. 2. Woman air pilots--United
States--Biography--Juvenile literature. [1. Earhart, Amelia, 1897-1937. 2. Air pilots. 3.
Woman--Biography.] I. Title. II. Series.

TL540.E3 B85 2000
629.13'092--dc21
[B]
                                                        99-042513

Color reproduction by Colourscan, Singapore
Printed and bound in Belgium by Proost

The publisher would like to thank the following for their
kind permission to reproduce their photographs:
Key: t=top; a=above; b=below; l=left; r=right; c=center
Ace Photo Agency: Front jacket; **Brown Brothers**: 22b, 33b, 36-37;
Corbis UK Ltd: Front jacket, 4cla, 6tl, 8cl, 11br, 11t, 20tl, 20bl, 21b,
25br, 27b, 31tr, 31cr, 32tl, 34b, 39t, 42tl, 46bl; **The Granger
Collection, New York**: 26tl; **Hulton Getty**: 2br, 9cra, 10tl, 10bl, 12bl,
14tl, 15br, 19tr, 19br, 21cr, 25t, 34tl, 41br; **Mary S Lovell**: 6clb, 19t,
38b, 40b, 46br, 47crb; **Popperfoto**: Reuters 43tr, 45tr; **Telegraph
Colour Library**: 18tl, 46tl; Ian McKinnell 36tl; J. Reardon 18cl;
Masterfile 21tr, 44bl; **Topham Picturepoint**: 30.

Grateful acknowledgment to Mary S. Lovell for the loan of photographs
used in her book *The Sound of Wings: The Biography of Amelia Earhart*

Contents

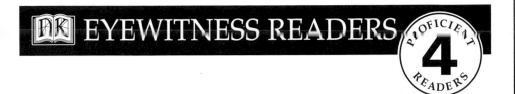

DK EYEWITNESS READERS

PROFICIENT
4
READERS

FLYING ACE

THE STORY OF
AMELIA EARHART

Written by Angela Bull

DK PUBLISHING, INC.

Roller coaster girl

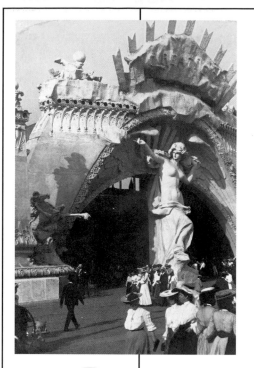

Amelia Earhart gazed up at the roller coaster. Its steep, looping curves seemed almost to touch the sky. Amelia tensed with excitement.

"I want to ride on it!" she cried. Her mother looked doubtful. Amelia was only seven.

"I'm not going to," said Amelia's four-year old sister, Muriel. "You'll have to try it without me."

Then Amelia's father came to the rescue.

"I'll take you, Amelia," he said. "We shouldn't miss it. Here we are at the St. Louis World's Fair and this roller coaster ride looks like more fun than anything."

Father and daughter got into the car and then jolted to a start. Slowly they climbed the first curve.

World's fair
The St Louis World's Fair in Missouri showed treasures from all over the world. The fair looked like a mini city full of palaces and fountains. But it was a temporary attraction and was taken down in 1904 after just seven months.

Then they plunged down faster and faster. Amelia screamed with delight. How silly of Mother and Muriel to stay on the ground, she thought. They could be whirling through the air like her.

Her eyes shone as she climbed out after the ride.

"It's like flying!" she exclaimed. Little did she know, Amelia had found the way in which one day she would become world-famous.

Keeping cool
The fair was held in hot weather and gallons of ice cream were sold. To make it easy to eat, the first edible cones were invented.

Train travel
Steam trains first appeared in the U.S. in the 1820s. They had dining cars and sleeping cars for rich passengers.

Birthplace
Amelia's grandparents' house still stands above the fast-flowing Missouri River. It is now the Amelia Earhart Museum.

The Earharts returned to Kansas City, where Amelia's father worked in a railroad office.

"Let's make our own roller coaster," Amelia suggested.

With the help of Muriel and an uncle she built a wooden track which she nailed to the shed roof. Next she found a small cart and hauled it up onto the roof.

Amelia scrambled on board and zoomed down the track. The moment she landed she jumped out and hauled the cart back to the roof. The sense of flying was wonderful.

Amelia's whole life was a bit like a roller coaster, with its ups and downs. She was born in 1897 at her grandparents' lovely home in Atchison, Kansas.

She lived there for much of the time with her mother, sister, and wealthy grandparents.

But she often went to live with her father in his poorer home near his job in Kansas City. Amelia's mother resented her husband's lack of money and his habit of drinking too much. She stayed away from him for months at a time.

No alcohol
Drinking problems caused misery to many families. In 1917 the U.S. government voted in favor of prohibition – an alcohol ban.

First flight
The first hot-air balloon to carry people was launched in France in 1783.

First plane
In 1903 Orville and Wilbur Wright built a plane called *Flyer*. In it they made the first controlled powered flight. It lasted just 12 seconds.

Amelia was an adventurous, active girl who liked to ride, skate, and shoot. She and Muriel attended a good school and learned to be polite and well-mannered.

Amelia was still a child when she saw her first airplane at the Iowa State Fair. Planes were still new inventions then. They were tiny, unsafe constructions covered in canvas. They could not go very far or very high. Amelia was not impressed. "Just rusty wire and wood," she would later say.

Amelia's grandfather died. Then later, when Amelia was fourteen, her grandmother died too.

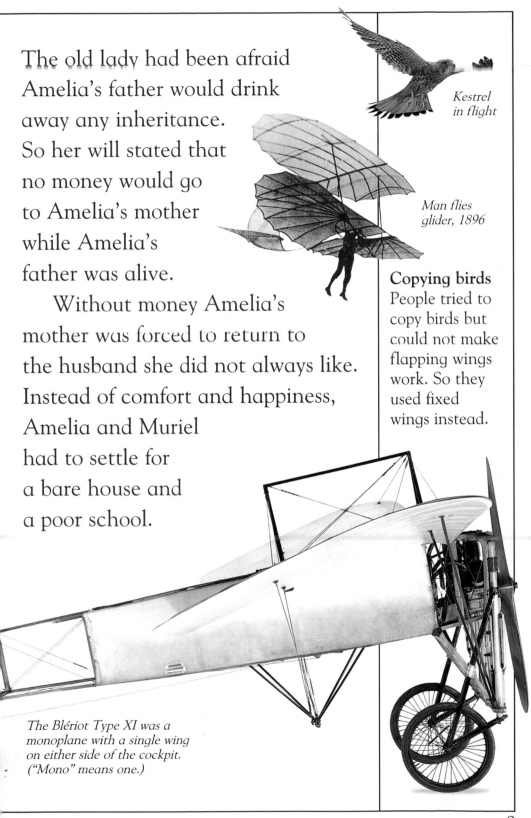

The old lady had been afraid Amelia's father would drink away any inheritance. So her will stated that no money would go to Amelia's mother while Amelia's father was alive.

Without money Amelia's mother was forced to return to the husband she did not always like. Instead of comfort and happiness, Amelia and Muriel had to settle for a bare house and a poor school.

Kestrel in flight

Man flies glider, 1896

Copying birds
People tried to copy birds but could not make flapping wings work. So they used fixed wings instead.

The Blériot Type XI was a monoplane with a single wing on either side of the cockpit. ("Mono" means one.)

Woman's work
Mary Pickford was a star of silent films. She played so many love scenes she was known as "America's sweetheart."

Nickname
U.S. soldiers were called "doughboys" because their uniform buttons looked like dough cakes.

As her life changed, Amelia changed too. There was no fun at home for a penniless family. Her father was often too drunk to take her to parties and other places. She missed her old friends and became a loner.

She knew she would have to fight her own way out of the misery. Maybe the best way was to study for a good job. Amelia worked hard at school, and read and wrote poetry.

Most girls at that time did not worry about careers. They planned to marry and have children. Amelia wanted more than that. She searched through newspapers for stories of women with good careers. She knew women could achieve as much as men. She wondered what her own career would be.

Amelia went to college as World War I raged in Europe. She read about the gruesome horrors of war.

Soldiers wore masks to protect them from poison gas.

Thousands of soldiers were wounded and killed by shells, bullets, and poison gas.

U.S. and Canadian soldiers were among those suffering terrible injuries. Amelia was concerned and wanted to help. Her classmates were not surprised when Amelia decided that nursing wounded men was more important than studying.

Taking care
Nurses looked after wounded, dying soldiers in the flimsy huts of field hospitals. Soldiers were sent back to the fighting if they got better.

During World War I pilots used tricky moves to avoid enemy fire. The Immelmann Turn was a steep climbing maneuver.

Famous pilot
"The Red Baron" was a German pilot. He fixed a machine gun to the front of his plane and shot down 80 aircraft before being shot down himself.

Amelia moved to Toronto, Canada, and spent almost a year working in a military hospital as a nursing aide. She scrubbed floors and handed out medicine and food. She worked long hours and grew pale and thin.

It was a great treat when, one day, three military pilots took her to see the planes at a nearby airfield. The planes were small and fragile, but hundreds of them were used in the war. And the best pilots were famous figures.

Amelia's nursing job ended soon after the war ended in November 1918. Military pilots also lost their jobs and many bought unwanted air force planes. They used them to earn money at air shows.

In those days flying was a new and exciting entertainment.

Ordinary people rarely saw a plane and few had the chance to fly. Air shows were popular – crowds gasped as pilots performed aerial rolls, wing walking, and parachute jumps.

Amelia too was thrilled by the air displays. She could see flying was dangerous, but it fascinated her.

Down to earth
Not all pilots survived air-show stunts. But they had more chances than World War I pilots. Every night there were empty places at air-base dinner tables. These belonged to war pilots who did not come back.

Taking control
U.S. women, including Elizabeth Cady Stanton, fought for the right to vote in elections. They finally won the right in 1920.

For Christmas 1920 the Earharts gathered in Los Angeles, California. Amelia's father had stopped drinking and her parents were trying to make a new, happy life together.

Amelia and her father visited an air show at Long Beach. As Amelia watched the planes swoop and dive she felt a chill of excitement. She realized then what she wanted. She wanted to fly!

But this was 1920. Women were expected to look after husbands and homes and nothing more.

Flying was rough and dangerous. Planes were primitive, unsafe, and often crashed. Yet Amelia felt strangely drawn to flying. Her father agreed that she could take a short flight.

Amelia was flushed with excitement as the pilot took off. From high in the sky she could see the ocean and the Hollywood hills. The sight was so inspiring she was sure she wanted to be a pilot.

Famous sign
The original Hollywood sign said "Hollywoodland" and advertised a housing development.

Fashion
In the 1920s women's fashion discarded long dresses and waist-squeezing corsets. Young women became flappers and wore dresses that showed their legs.

Going forward
Engines are used to power propellers. These mini spinning wings thrust a plane forward.

But how could Amelia learn to fly? Try Neta Snook, she was told. Neta gave lessons.

Neta, one of the few woman pilots, watched Amelia walk toward her. Amelia wore a smart suit and white gloves. Neta eyed the unsuitable clothes doubtfully, but still she agreed to give Amelia a lesson the following day.

Dressed now in riding breeches, Amelia climbed into the dual-control plane.

Neta talked to Amelia about flying. Then she taught her to taxi across the ground and take off. Suddenly Amelia was in the air! She felt wonderful. Neta was impressed. Very few people learned how to fly a plane as quickly as Amelia had.

In fact Amelia's reckless confidence was alarming. She soared upward or dived beneath high-tension wires without showing any fear.

After a few days Amelia bought a leather coat to cover her smart clothes. It soon became creased and oil-stained as Amelia hung around the airfield finding out how airplanes worked. Everything to do with flying and planes was interesting to her. Amelia was happy now that she had found her purpose in life.

Wood work
Early propellers were made of wood. Some war-plane propellers were covered in brass to protect them from enemy fire.

Plane safety
Air lanes, or invisible roads in the sky, have been used since 1922. Pilots are given specific times they can fly these routes to prevent mid-air crashes.

Up in the air
Air-traffic controllers direct thousands of planes that take off and land each day. They make sure a runway is clear for each plane.

Once Amelia could fly, she wanted her own plane. She took odd jobs, saved every penny, and borrowed what she could. By her middle twenties she had raised enough money to buy a tiny plane. It was called *Canary* because it was painted bright yellow.

Neta, who was still flying with Amelia, thought the plane was too light to be safe. It was not a good plane for a beginner. However, Amelia was determined to have it.

In her early flying days Amelia had several small accidents. They scared other people, but Amelia was not worried about them.

Once she crashed *Canary* as she was taking off. Amelia bit her tongue but was otherwise unhurt. She crawled out of the damaged plane, then powdered her nose.

Neta Snook and Amelia in California

Rudolph Valentino

A plane crash – even a minor one – was a big news story in 1921. Amelia told Neta they must look nice in case a newspaper reporter arrived to interview them.

Later that year Amelia made her first solo flight. The takeoff was awkward, but she managed it. Then she flew up high over the airfield. Amelia was happy. Now she was free to be alone in the sky as much and as often as she liked.

Charlie Chaplin

First taste of fame

Record breaker
Lindbergh crossed the Atlantic in a plane that was built for him in just two months. It was called *The Spirit of St. Louis* because St. Louis businessmen financed the flight.

Charles Lindbergh

In May 1927 Charles Lindbergh became the first person to fly solo across the Atlantic. He stayed awake for over 33 hours to fly his plane.

Instantly he became a celebrity. Other people tried to copy his feat, but only four succeeded while 14 died in crashes.

Lindbergh's publicity was masterminded by George Putnam. Putnam was a publisher specializing in real-life adventures.

After Lindbergh's flight, a rich American named Amy Guest contacted Putnam. She wanted to sponsor the first woman to fly the Atlantic. She asked Putnam to find "the right sort of girl." This meant someone attractive and confident enough to handle the fame that would follow.

Friends told Putnam about Amelia and he invited her for an interview.

Amelia charmed him, so Putnam offered her the Atlantic flight. She would not fly the plane herself – a professional pilot would handle that. Amelia would be the captain. She would keep the log, writing in it what happened during the flight.

The plan must be kept secret in case another woman heard and made the crossing first.

Concorde
This modern-day plane travels faster than the speed of sound. It crosses the Atlantic in less than three hours.

Amelia and George Putnam planned the flight in detail.

Ocean liner
In the 1920s it took five days to cross the Atlantic by ship. Some ships were like luxury hotels with swimming pools, movie theaters, and ballrooms.

Plane sailing
Seaplanes sit on floats and take off and land on water. They have rudders at the back so they can be steered on water.

Amelia agreed to make the journey. She heard the plane was called *Friendship*. It had pontoon floats instead of wheels in case it had to come down in the water.

Friendship was moored in Boston Harbor. Amelia and the other two crew members boarded it from a tugboat. The pilot, Bill Stultz, climbed into his seat at the front of the plane. He started the engines, then *Friendship* lumbered into the air.

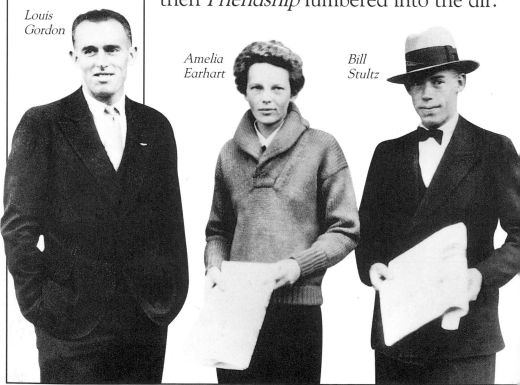

Louis Gordon

Amelia Earhart

Bill Stultz

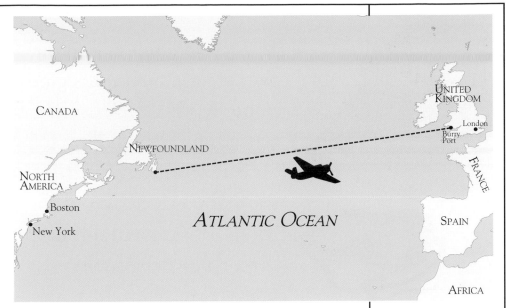

Amelia's route across the Atlantic Ocean in 1928

They flew to Newfoundland where the trans-Atlantic flight would begin. But in Newfoundland bad weather grounded them. For 13 days the crew was stuck. The wait was frustrating, tedious, and stressful. Stultz coped by drinking too much.

Amelia took command. She made Stultz drink black coffee until he was sober. And she insisted on leaving the moment the weather was clear. So on June 17, 1928, they boarded the plane again. *Friendship* spluttered upward. The crossing had begun!

Deadly waters
The Northern Atlantic is freezing cold. It was here that the *Titanic* hit an iceberg in 1912. The ship sank with a loss of 1523 lives.

Dress sense
Early planes did not always have covered cockpits. Pilots wore warm leather coats, helmets, and gloves. Goggles protected their eyes from biting winds. Some goggles were tinted to reduce glare.

Up, up, and on and on they flew. Amelia was glad of her leather coat as they passed through chilling fog.

Suddenly they hit a snowstorm. Ice covered the wings. Stultz went into a dive, throwing Amelia across the cabin.

Day turned into night and night into day. The radio stopped working. Fuel was low. They should have sighted land by now.

Several ships cut across their path. They circled over one ship and Amelia dropped messages. The notes asked for their position. But the messages fell into the ocean and were lost.

All three peered through the windows, anxious and tense. Suddenly Bill's face lit up in a smile! He could see land ahead.

The relief was enormous. Bill made a perfect landing in the sea near Burry Port in Wales. He went ashore first and phoned the press. By the time Amelia reached land, she was famous. Two thousand people rushed to see her.

On her way home Amelia was welcomed in London. In New York George Putnam organized a ticker-tape parade for her, with torn paper thrown at her open car.

Homecoming
A ticker-tape parade was a traditional welcome for a hero in New York.

The Atlantic – solo

Black Tuesday
In 1929 prices on the U.S. stock market crashed. Some people lost everything.

1930 brides
Most women married in their early twenties, so at 33 Amelia seemed old.

Amelia was aware she had only been a passenger on *Friendship*. Any woman could have done it. She felt she needed an achievement of her own. After the flight she was well paid for public appearances. So in 1929, a year when many were short of money, Amelia bought a new plane, a Lockheed Vega.

In 1931 she married George Putnam. He had managed her publicity and advised her on her speeches and clothes. They spent time together and had grown close.

With her private life settled, Amelia began planning her great adventure. "Would you mind if I flew the Atlantic alone?" she asked Putnam one morning.

Putnam did not mind, in fact he was enthusiastic. A solo crossing by a woman would set a new record.

Amelia could write a book and earn a lot of money. Putnam decided that May 20, 1932, would be the ideal day. It was the fifth anniversary of Lindbergh's crossing.

Air race
In 1929 Amelia also organized a women's cross-country air race. It was dubbed "The Powder-Puff Derby."

Night flying
Pilots used the instrument panel for safe flying. The panel had an altimeter to show the plane's height and an artificial horizon to show if the plane was going up, down, or side to side.

As the day neared, Amelia flew to Newfoundland, her starting point. She knew she risked her life, but she wanted to prove a woman could make the journey.

She took off safely, then as night fell her altimeter failed. Without it Amelia could not tell if she was a safe distance above the ocean. She was in danger, but she kept going.

She flew into a storm. Flames spurted from a cracked exhaust pipe. Amelia was cold and frightened, but she did not turn back.

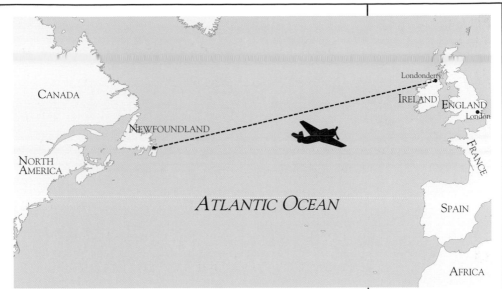

Amelia's solo route across the Atlantic Ocean in 1932

Amelia climbed to avoid clouds. Then ice formed on the wings. Suddenly the plane spun downward! Down and down it fell, with Amelia desperately trying to regain control. After a 3,000-foot drop Amelia righted the plane. Just in time!

But then the fuel gauge jammed and fumes filled the cockpit. Dizzy and unsure of her fuel, she knew she had to land soon.

Then she saw a wonderful sight. There was land right beneath her! Amelia had made the crossing.

Downward spin
Air-show pilots perform spins by flying slowly. When air flows too slowly over the wings the plane "stalls" and falls toward earth.

29

THE ILLUSTRATED LONDON NEWS

The Copyright of all the Editorial Matter, both Engravings and Letterpress, is Strictly Reserved in Great Britain, the Colonies, Europe, and the United States of America.

SATURDAY, MAY 28, 1932.

THE FIRST WOMAN TO FLY THE ATLANTIC ALONE: MISS AMELIA EARHART AND HER 'PLANE AT CULMORE, NEAR LONDONDERRY, WHERE SHE WAS FORCED TO LAND.

Miss Amelia Earhart (Mrs. G. P. Putnam), the famous American airwoman, flying from Harbour Grace, Newfoundland, with Paris as her destination, had to land in a ten-acre field at Culmore, some two miles from Londonderry, Northern Ireland, on May 21. Thus she did not carry out her intention to the last, but she set up a record by being the first woman to make a lone flight across the Atlantic—in which connection it is interesting to note that her feat took place on the fifth anniversary of the solo Atlantic-crossing by Lindbergh. The third pilot who has made a solo crossing by air is Squadron-Leader Bert Hinkler. Miss Earhart has now flown the Atlantic twice—another record. On the first occasion, which was in June 1928, she was a passenger with Messrs. Wilmer Stultz and Louis Gordon. The airwoman spent the night in Ireland. On the following day, the Sunday, she was conveyed by air to Blackpool, and thence to Hanworth.

The next day Amelia taxied her plane around the field for news cameras. She climbed out and the crowd threw hats in the air. Newsfilm of this was shown at movie theaters. It was said to be Amelia's actual landing.

She landed in a field, where a man was herding cows. He told her she was near Londonderry in Ireland. He was astonished when she said she had come from America.

30

Amelia telephoned Putnam who alerted the press. As Amelia traveled home through Ireland and England, excited people mobbed her. In London her plane was displayed in Selfridges department store.

Back in the United States Putnam organized more lectures and public appearances for Amelia. She got involved in running new airlines and designing clothes for active living. She was a real celebrity, even staying at the White House with President Roosevelt and his wife.

Amelia was one of the best-known women in America. But by the age of 35 she was worried about how quickly she could react when flying. She was afraid she might be slowing down.

She wanted to make another big trip to prove to everyone that she was still as good as ever.

The President Franklin D. Roosevelt's social reforms helped many U.S. families.

Talking point Amelia was friendly with Eleanor, the president's wife. Eleanor spoke out for women's rights.

Amy Johnson
This pilot was the first woman to fly solo from England to Australia. On route she fixed her plane's torn canvas wings with adhesive bandages.

Crackups

After the Atlantic crossing, Amelia never received as much praise again. With the passing of time, flying was no longer such a novelty. Other women pilots broke records too. Amelia was not quite as special as she used to be.

Amelia's next long solo flight was from Hawaii to California. The takeoff from Hawaii was terrible. The Vega was weighed down with fuel. Its wheels sank in the mud before the plane jolted upward.

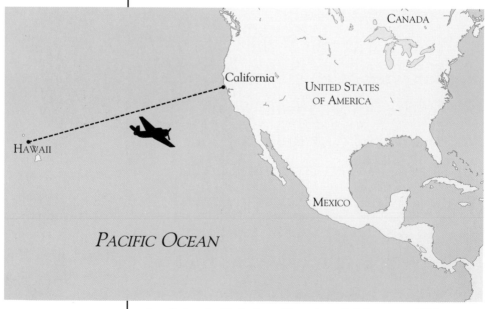

Amelia's solo flight from Hawaii to California in 1935

Amelia lost her way and had to ask a ship below for her location. When she eventually landed in California she was thankful to climb out of the cockpit alive.

Critics said the flight had only been a publicity stunt to attract attention. They thought the poor takeoff and faulty navigation showed that she was not in full control of her plane. Her days as a heroine seemed over.

Amelia climbing into the cockpit of her Lockheed Vega

Navigation aid
A compass has a dial marked north, south, east, and west. It also has a magnetic needle that always points northward. Navigators use compasses to work out where they are.

Wind factor
In Amelia's day wind made navigation difficult. It could blow a plane off course or make it travel faster or slower than the speed shown on the instrument-panel dials.

Time to think
Simone de Beauvoir was a French philosopher. She believed that women let themselves be governed by men and set down her ideas in a book called *The Second Sex*.

Although her flight from Hawaii had been criticized, Amelia never dreamed of giving up flying. Her achievements were not just for herself. Flying was her way of showing that women could do the same things that men did.

Putnam still organized lecture tours and media interviews for Amelia so people remembered her.

Amelia spoke to the press throughout her career.

34

Amelia wanted to be known. But she realized that she needed new achievements to keep up her position as a famous woman pilot.

Amelia had had five "crackups," as she called crashes, but not even these were enough to stop her flying. Luckily she had never been badly injured and her planes had always been repaired. Now, with the flight from Hawaii behind her, Amelia began to consider what she would try next.

She wanted to do something new. She began to plan a flight that no one had attempted before. She wanted to be the first woman to fly around the world along its widest point, from east to west.

Amelia's attempted flight around the world from east to west in March 1937

North America
California
HAWAII
HOWLAND ISLAND
Equator
SOUTH AMERICA
PACIFIC OCEAN

The equator
This is an imaginary line around the widest part of the globe. It is 24,901.8 miles (40,076 km) long. The equator is the hottest part of the earth because it is closest to the sun.

Setting course
The sun rises in the east and sets in the west. Navigators used the sun to work out directions by day. At night they used stars.

After its tough journey, Amelia's Vega had dangerously cracked wings. She was lucky to still be alive! With her savings, Amelia bought herself a new plane. It was a big, powerful Lockheed Electra.

The Electra had extra gasoline tanks, better radio equipment, and a hatch through which a navigator could steer by the sun and stars.

Unfortunately Amelia never mastered the radio equipment.

Nor did she know enough of the beeps of Morse code to transmit messages. The day would soon come when she would regret these failings.

Amelia got the Electra on her thirty-ninth birthday and spent five weeks in practice flights. She found the plane and its equipment difficult to handle.

News of Amelia's proposed flight leaked out, but Amelia denied it. "All applesauce!" she declared airily. She could not risk a rival pilot making the flight before her.

SOS

• • • — — — • • •

Coded message
Morse code uses dots and dashes that can be tapped out. Different combinations stand for different numbers and letters. Three dots, three dashes, then three more dots represents SOS, a call for help.

NR
16020

Amelia's Lockheed Electra 10E had its registration code on the tail.

Coral islands
Many small islands in the Pacific are made by marine creatures called corals. New corals grow on old, forming solid island structures.

So Amelia secretly prepared for her first attempt to fly around the world. She would travel from California to Hawaii to tiny Howland Island. From there she would continue her westward journey all the way back to America.

Amelia decided to take three crew members on the first stage of the journey. She needed expert help to find Howland Island so she chose navigator Fred Noonan.

Paul Mantz, Amelia Earhart, Harry Manning, and Fred Noonan before the around-the-world attempt

Irish saint's day
Amelia took off for Hawaii on March 17, 1937, St. Patrick's Day. Noonan wore a shamrock to celebrate his Irish ancestry.

When Amelia was ready Putnam alerted the press. They watched a successful takeoff from Oakland Airfield in California. After 15 hours and 51 minutes Amelia and her crew landed safely in Hawaii.

After refueling Amelia was ready to take off again. But the plane swayed down the runway then tilted over. A wing smashed, a wheel broke off. The Electra stopped and Amelia emerged, white-faced.

Noonan calmly folded his maps. He would be ready to go again whenever Amelia wanted, he stated.

But the Electra was too badly damaged to fly. This around-the-world flight was over.

Strong wheels
Early planes used car wheels for takeoff and landing. Then, as planes became heavier, pressed-steel wheels were used. Wheels were also positioned father apart so the planes would not topple over.

Amelia left
Putnam a letter.
In it she wrote,
"Women must
try to do things
as men have
tried. When
they fail, their
failure must be
but a challenge
to others."

Into the blue

The failed attempt only made
Amelia more determined to fly
around the world. Huge oceans
and hot tangled jungles would not
stop her. Refueling on primitive
runways would not put her off.

Putnam
agreed that she
should try again.
However, this
time she would
fly west to east.
This would leave
the difficult
Pacific crossing
until she felt
completely in
control of her
plane. Noonan
agreed to go too.

On May 21,
1937, the Electra
was ready.

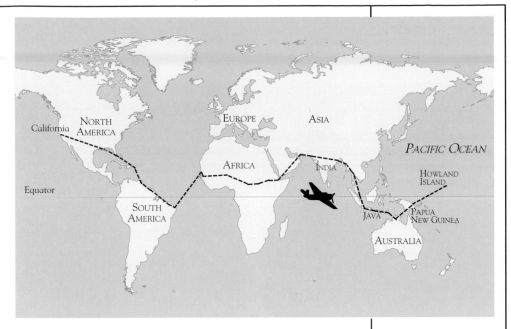

Amelia's flight around the world from west to east in June 1937

Amelia flew eastward from California to Miami, Florida.

In Miami, Amelia discarded some Morse equipment because neither she nor Noonan could operate it. She also left behind the extra radio equipment that she had not needed on her previous trips.

Amelia was afraid this second around-the-world flight may fail. She dreaded growing old and told a reporter, "I won't feel completely cheated if I fail to come back."

Radio message
A microphone turns the sound of a voice into an electric signal. This is sent to the receiver. When the caller says "over" the other person can speak.

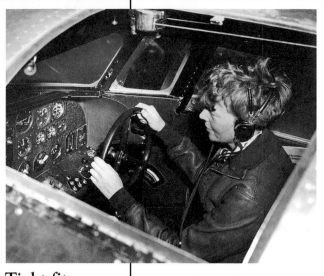

On June 1, 1937, Amelia took off from Miami airport. She and Noonan flew to South America, then across to Africa.

Tight fit
Amelia's cockpit measured less than 5 ft (1.5 m) in any direction

Bedbugs
These feed on human and animal blood. Young bedbugs are almost see-through. But they turn dark red after a good meal of blood.

The plane was cramped and noisy. Noonan sat at a map table behind the cockpit. When he wanted to communicate with Amelia he passed her messages on the end of a fishing line. It was easier than trying to shout.

They crossed Africa, where storms and headwinds made it difficult to hold the plane on course. When they landed they slept in primitive airfields. Amelia and Noonan were hot, uncomfortable, and bitten raw by bedbugs.

Even though Noonan was with her, Amelia felt alone. Gasoline fumes in the cockpit made her sick, and she grew very tired.

They pressed on over India, where they battled with monsoon rains. When they reached Java after three weeks and twenty thousand miles, Amelia was exhausted. She was thankful to stop while the plane was overhauled. There were still another nine thousand miles to go.

Monsoon rains
Monsoon winds bring torrential rains to India. These often cause floods. The monsoon starts in May and dies down in October.

Putnam planned for Amelia to land back in the United States on the Fourth of July. He even arranged for her to broadcast from San Francisco on July 5. Amelia knew this was impossible.

She flew from Java to Lae, in Papua New Guinea. This was the takeoff point for the final part of her journey across the Pacific.

Then on July 2 she left Lae. Watchers saw the Electra for the last time as it lumbered into the clouds. It was heavily laden with fuel. Its destination was tiny Howland Island.

Amelia and Noonan had only a basic idea of how to use the radio.

Yet for the Pacific crossing Amelia had to communicate with the Coast Guard cutter *Itasca*. This ship would give her locations and weather reports.

The *Itasca* tried to guide her, but Amelia seemed unable to hear its transmissions. At last Amelia's voice crackled through the static. She was not sure where she was, she told them, and fuel was low.

Through the early hours of July 3 the *Itasca* picked up messages of increasing desperation. Then there was silence. No one ever heard from Amelia or Noonan again.

Sea patrol
Coast guards work on ships and wear uniforms, like sailors in the navy. But coast guards have their own jobs to do, including searching ships for smuggled goods, weapons, and drugs.

Pacific islands
There are many uninhabited islands in the Pacific. Palms grow beside beautiful empty beaches. But behind the beaches vines twist into dense jungle. The waters around the islands are full of sharks.

What had happened to Amelia? The most probable answer was that the Electra ran out of fuel and crashed into the Pacific. A huge search-and-rescue operation was launched involving nine naval ships and over 60 planes.

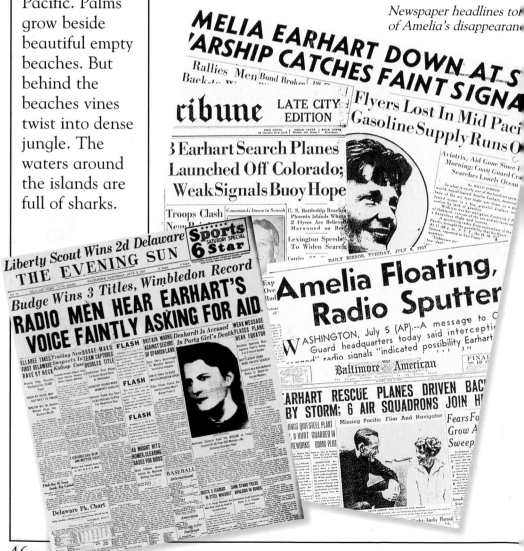

Newspaper headlines tol of Amelia's disappearanc

One ship searched for wreckage along what was thought to be the Electra's flight path. Faint radio signals were reported, apparently coming from islands 350 miles (560 km) southeast of Howland.

Airplanes surveyed the islands, but found nothing – or almost nothing. One plane spotted "traces of recent habitation" on Gardner Island, but no Amelia.

Amelia was so famous that the mystery could not be forgotten. A theory surfaced that she was spying on Japan for the U.S. government. She had been shot down, imprisoned, killed. But no evidence for this was ever produced.

Perhaps Amelia did crash onto Gardner Island. We may never know. She was a brave, record-breaking pilot who showed what women were capable of. And her disappearance remains a mystery.

Radio messages
Hoaxers tried to join the action. They sent made-up messages from Amelia.

Flight recorder
Today's black box, which is in fact orange, records what the crew says.

Stamp out
Amelia continued to be famous. In 1964 a stamp was issued in her memory.

Glossary

Aerial rolls
When aircraft rotate sideways without losing height or direction.

Black box
A flight recorder used by people investigating a plane crash.

Cockpit
This houses the flight instruments used by a pilot.

Compass
An instrument with a magnetic needle that is used to find directions.

Crew
The people in charge of a plane, including the pilot and navigator.

Cutter
A small, fast boat used by the Coast Guard.

Dive
A steep, nose-down descent by a plane during which speed builds up rapidly.

Dual-control plane
A plane with two sets of controls. A learner uses one set. The instructor can take charge by using the other.

Equator
An imaginary line around the globe an equal distance from the north and south poles.

Flight path
The course of an aircraft through the air.

Headwinds
Winds that blow directly against the course of an aircraft.

Hot-air balloon
A balloon that rises when the air inside it is heated. It flies because hot air is lighter than cold air.

Log
The detailed record of an aircraft's journey.

Microphone
A device that picks up sound and transmits it in electrical waves.

Morse code
A code system in which letters and numbers are represented by dots and dashes and transmitted by sound signals.

Navigation
The process of working out the route an aircraft should take.

Parachute
A giant canopy that slows a person falling to earth.

Pontoon floats
Watertight, box-like attachments under a seaplane that enable it to float.

Propeller
A twisted wood or metal plane part. It spins at the front of a plane and thrusts the plane forward.

Publicity stunt
A method of gaining public attention for a person or thing.

Publisher
A person who turns an author's written work into a printed book.

Rudder
The flat steering equipment at the back of a plane or boat.

Social reforms
Measures taken to improve people's lives including better schools and pensions.

Spin
A spiral nose dive.

Ticker tape
Paper ribbons used to record stock prices.

Transmission
A message sent through radio waves.

Tugboat
A small powerful boat used to tow craft at sea.

Women's rights
The concept of giving women the same rights and pay as men.

EYEWITNESS READERS

Level 1
Beginning to Read

A Day at Greenhill Farm
Truck Trouble
Tale of a Tadpole
Surprise Puppy!
Duckling Days
A Day at Seagull Beach
Whatever the Weather
Busy Buzzy Bee
Big Machines
Wild Baby Animals
LEGO: Trouble at the Bridge

Level 2
Beginning to Read Alone

Dinosaur Dinners
Fire Fighter!
Bugs! Bugs! Bugs!
Slinky, Scaly Snakes!
Animal Hospital
The Little Ballerina
Munching, Crunching, Sniffing,
    and Snooping
The Secret Life of Trees
Winking, Blinking, Wiggling,
    and Waggling
Astronaut – Living in Space
LEGO: Castle Under Attack!

Level 3
Reading Alone

Spacebusters
Beastly Tales
Shark Attack!
Titanic
Invaders from Outer Space
Movie Magic
Plants Bite Back!
Time Traveler
Bermuda Triangle
Tiger Tales
Aladdin
Heidi
LEGO: Mission to the Arctic

Level 4
Proficient Readers

Days of the Knights
Volcanoes
Secrets of the Mummies
Pirates!
Horse Heroes
Trojan Horse
Micromonsters
Going for Gold!
Extreme Machines
Flying Ace – The Story of
    Amelia Earhart
Robin Hood
Black Beauty
LEGO: Race for Survival